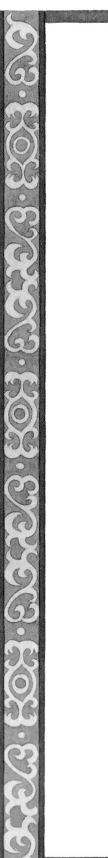

THE
WAITING DAY

BY

HARRIETT DILLER

ILLUSTRATIONS BY

CHI CHUNG

GREEN TIGER PRESS

Published by Simon & Schuster

New York London Toronto Sydney Tokyo Singapore

GREEN TIGER PRESS

1230 Avenue of the Americas, New York, New York 10020

Text copyright © 1994 by Harriett Diller

Illustrations copyright © 1994 by Chi Chung

All rights reserved including the right of reproduction

in whole or in part in any form.

GREEN TIGER PRESS and colophon are registered trademarks

of Simon & Schuster.

Designed by Alan Benjamin and Paul Zakris.

The text for this book is set in 14-point Palatino.

The illustrations were done in watercolor.

Manufactured in the United States of America.

10 9 8 7 6 5 4 3 2 1

Library of Congress Cataloging-in-Publication Data

Diller, Harriett.

   The waiting day / by Harriett Diller ; illustrated by Chi Chung

     p. cm.

   Summary: A busy ferryman who works hard to please his

demanding and unappreciative passengers learns an important

lesson from a beggar sitting patiently by the riverbank.

   [1. Conduct of life—Fiction. 2. Ferries—Fiction.

3. Beggars—Fiction.] I. Chung, Chi, ill. II. Title.

PZ7.D5774Wai 1994   [E]—dc20 93-16785 CIP AC

ISBN: 0-671-86579-X

To Jeff
—H. D.

To my parents, Mr. and Mrs. K. M. Chung,
with love and appreciation
—C. C.

The ferryman first noticed the old man at daybreak. He sat hunched on the riverbank as the ferryman readied his raft for the day's journeys.

"A beggar, no doubt," he said to himself, "waiting for free passage." It was the custom among the ferrymen on the long river to carry one beggar across each day without charge. "But he will have to wait for his free trip," the ferryman said to himself as a group of poets and scholars arrived on the riverbank.

"We must get to the other side," the poets and scholars told the ferryman, "to share our vast knowledge with the people on the far side of the river."

The ferryman was honored that such important people had chosen him, but this was also a problem. His simple wooden raft would never do for such distinguished passengers.

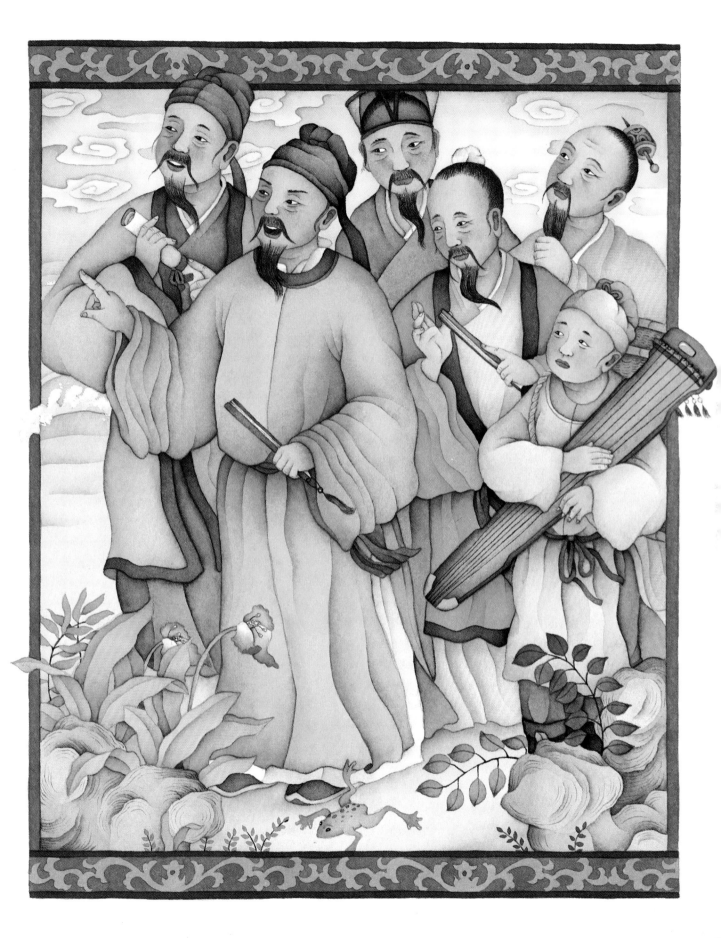

"We must cross the river in a t'e-chou," they told him.
So the ferryman made a little house out of sticks for
his wooden raft. It would keep the summer sun off
his distinguished passengers.

When the ferryman returned from his trip across
the river, the beggar was still squatting on the bank.
"He will have to wait for his free ride until I am
ready," the ferryman muttered.

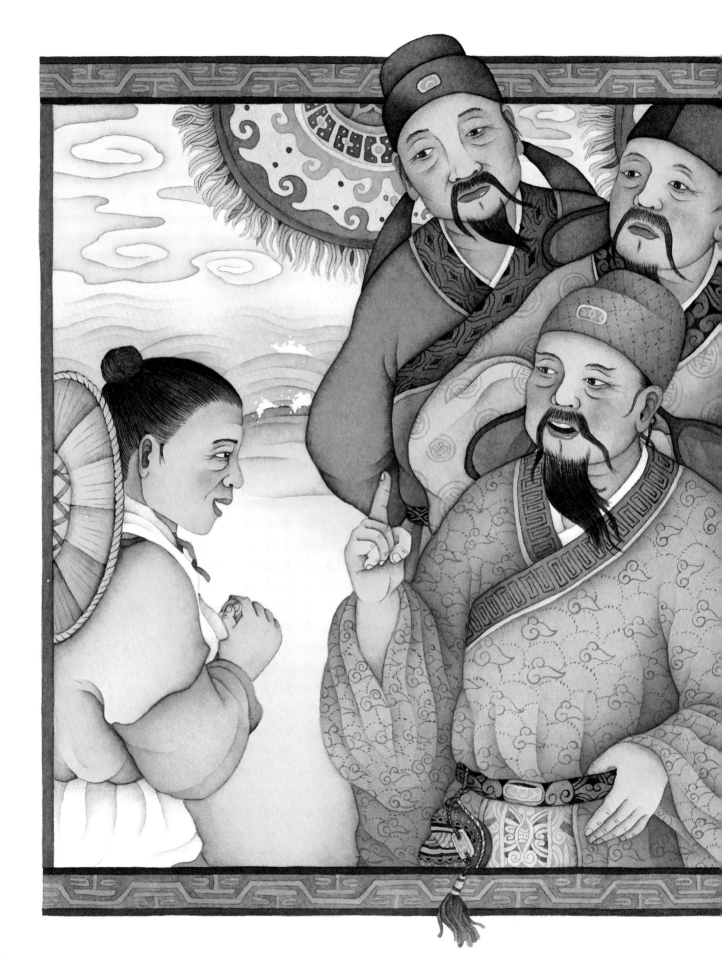

As the sun grew hotter, some government officials strode toward the ferryman and demanded to be taken across the river. "We must get to the other side at once," they snapped. "Important government business."

The ferryman went to work. Even the t'e-chou was not fancy enough for such outstanding people as these. The only proper way for government officials to cross the river was on a fang-chou, two boats roped together.

The ferryman tied another raft to his ferry, but the government officials were not satisfied with the fang-chou and the little house to keep off the sun.

"Have you nothing for us to eat on our journey?"
they said.

So the ferryman brought food aboard for the
passengers to eat.

It was early afternoon when the ferryman returned from his trip across the long river. He wondered how the old beggar could bear to wait on the sunny riverbank so long. "But wait he will if he expects a free ride today," he grumbled. "I am too busy to bother with him yet."

A bevy of lords and barons crowded around the ferryman. "We must cross to the other side," they commanded. "We have an important ceremony to attend."

The ferryman felt more and more important himself. Serving the lords and barons was such an honor that he did not even mind the dilemma that faced him now. This distinguished group of passengers required the most special boat yet—a wei-chou, four rafts tied together with ropes.

But the lords and barons were not satisfied with the wei-chou, the food, or the little house to keep off the sun. "Have you nothing to entertain us with on our journey?" they asked.

So the ferryman hired a group of musicians to play for the lords and barons.

Upon his return, the ferryman saw that the old beggar still waited. "Why should I carry a beggar across the river on this fancy wei-chou?" he asked himself.

The ferryman was just about to ask the beggar this question when he was startled by the blare of a trumpet.

A man stepped forward and announced, "The emperor must get to the other side of the river to inspect his new land."

The ferryman set to work in a frenzy. There was only one suitable way for the emperor to cross the river—by a pontoon bridge. And the only way to create such a bridge was to tie together all the rafts on the river.

The ferryman gathered the rafts. He looked at the little house of sticks. He smelled the fragrant plates of food. He listened to the music. He saw the rafts stretching all the way across the wide water like a long wooden bridge. Surely the emperor would be impressed by such splendor.

But the emperor only snorted. "Have you no throne? Do you expect me to walk across this bridge instead of being carried?"

So the tired ferryman set to work once more. He found
a chair to serve as a throne. He draped it with a beautiful
cloth. He helped carry the emperor across the river.

Worn out from his day's work, the ferryman was annoyed to find the old beggar still sitting on the riverbank.

"I suppose you have waited all day to cross the river," he snapped. "And I do not suppose you can pay."

The old man looked surprised. After a long pause he spoke. "You are right. I have waited all day—but not for your ferry."

"The most important people in the land use my ferry," protested the ferryman. "Poets and scholars. Government officials. Lords and barons. Even the emperor himself. Yet you, who are nothing but a beggar, do not wait to ride my ferry. What else could you possibly be waiting for?"

"To see the sunset," the old man said in a quiet voice.

The ferryman laughed. "You sat all day in the hot sun waiting to see the sunset? Did it never occur to you to wait until evening and then come to watch the sunset?"

"If I do not see the sun climb out of the river at daybreak, if I do not see the sun turn the river silver

at midday, if I do not see the sun become persimmon red as it drops toward the river in late afternoon, then I am not ready to see the sunset."

The ferryman stomped off to tie up his raft for the night. "As if I could not see the sunset if I wanted to. In fact, I will go do just that."

And the ferryman meant to, but he was so busy with other chores that he forgot all about the sunset until it was over. He turned back to the old beggar. "Well, I hope that the sunset was worth waiting for all day."

The old man smiled in the near darkness. "It was," he said. "It was." He struggled to his feet and walked slowly away.

The ferryman thought of all the people he
had seen that day: the poets and scholars, the
government officials, the lords and barons, the
emperor himself. Only the old beggar had waited
patiently. Only the old beggar had not asked

for more. Yet only the old beggar had seemed
satisfied.

"Please," the ferryman called to the old man, who
was just starting down the road, "tell me more about
this waiting."